SHARING

by Janet Riehecky
illustrated by Christina Rigo

Mankato, MN 56001

When my brother Tommy
sleeps in bed with me,
he doubles up
and makes
himself
exactly
like
a
V.
And 'cause the bed is not so wide,
a part of him is on my side.

—A. B. Ross
from *Two In Bed*

Library of Congress Cataloging in Publication Data

Riehecky, Janet, 1953
 Sharing.

 (What is it?)
 Summary: Suggests ways of sharing things with family and friends.
 1. Sharing—Juvenile literature. [1. Sharing]
I. Rigo, Christina Ljungren, ill. II. Title.
III. Series.
BJ1533.G4L36 1988   177'.7   87-36822
ISBN 0-89565-416-4 -1991 Edition

© 1988 The Child's World, Inc.
All rights reserved. Printed in U.S.A.

What is sharing?
Sometimes it's letting your little
brother sleep in bed with you.

Sharing is lending your friend
one of your buckets and a shovel. . .

and it's taking turns on the swing set.

When you're bouncing a ball,
and a friend comes over,

sharing is playing catch.

Sharing is giving half of your cookie to your best friend—even if it's your favorite, chocolate chip.

When you build a snow fort with your friends, you share the work...

and then you share the snowballs.

Sharing is giving—not only at Christmas. . .

but all year round.

When you play with the blocks at school, sharing is "one for you, and one for me."

You should also share when it's time to pick up.

Showing your classmates photographs and souvenirs from your summer vacation is sharing.

And you share your birthday joy when you give each classmate a special cupcake.

Sharing is telling Dad about your school trip to the petting zoo. . .

and then listening while your sister tells about her day.

When Mom reads a story, sharing is moving over and making room for your little brother.

And when you share the chicken pox
with your brother, you can also
share the TV.

Sometimes sharing is crying together—
like when your puppy is lost.

And sometimes sharing is a great, big hug.

Sharing is picking flowers to surprise your mom. . .

and sharing is telling your dad the secret.

Sharing makes others feel good,
and it makes you feel good too.